The Cuck, his Wife and her Boss

Sexy bedtime stories for adults

By Dante

Copyright © 2021 Dante

Contents

Introduction

I know it's not her fault, it was me, I encouraged her to let him seduce her. They're in our bedroom right now making love and I can hear everything... I've never been able to make her cum like that and I've lost count how many times. I don't know why but it turns me on so much knowing she's with another guy.

It all started a couple of months ago when she came home from work one evening and told me her boss had come on to her. She said nothing happened as we'd only been married a couple of years and even though, I couldn't satisfy her in bed, I know she loved me, and my below average size and premature ejaculation didn't bother her.

But him flirting with her turned me on so much, I couldn't stop thinking about it and asked her to tell me exactly what happened. She was a bit reluctant at first, but when I told her, I truly loved her and she saw how quickly I became aroused, she told me all the details and we made love passionately for the first time in over a year. Not that I lasted very long... in fact, I shot my load within the first few minutes, but was able to continue pleasuring her using my mouth and fingers, bringing her off as she also became aroused by telling me what happened.

And now we're in so deep, she's bringing him home to sleep in our bed as I lay awake all night in the spare room, listening to her moans and sighs. She leaves the door open slightly so I can hear and peep through the gap and he knows all about me.

I'd better start at the beginning as I'm so turned on and want to write this down. It all started when Kirsty my wife of two years started working at Barclays bank. She's 23, very attractive and a typical girl next door type with long dark brown hair, sexy size 10 figure and at 5 feet 8 has beautiful long legs. Her bottom and 34 B breasts are perfect and up until this all began, was very reserved and demure.

I'm Greg and slightly older at 28, fairly fit as I enjoy biking and cycle fifteen miles to work everyday. I work in a warehouse and met Kirsty when we were at a local community center, doing a course in alternative health.

So she's been working at Barclays in St Albans for about six months and told me, a new branch manager had been posted to her bank and started flirting with her. She was quite open about it as she's been totally faithful, as I am to her. But for whatever reason, like I said, it got me so turned on, I had to know more. She said, whenever nobody else was around, he would always be coming on to her and putting his arm around her shoulder, whispering comments about her looks. She said he's from Brazil and speaks very good English, well educated and in his late 50's. Obviously quite successful and drives a Mercedes SL sports.

So on this particular day, she and all the other staff, had to attend a training seminar in London and he'd offered to give her a lift home. She knew he was married so was really surprised when he put his hand on her leg as they were driving down the motorway, saying how sexy she looked and how he had a thing for stockings and pantyhose. She was wearing tights and her skirt was mid thigh, exposing her nylon covered legs. Not wanting to lose her job, she jokingly told him she was married and casually moved his hand away.

I asked her if it turned her on? And her response was, that it did, and she saw him touching his erection as he continued driving.

But she stressed that she loved me, and even when he did it again, this time blatantly caressing and squeezing her knee and leg, she moved him away again. She assured me nothing else happened, but realised I was incredibly turned on and we started making love. I couldn't stop thinking and talking about it and we made love again and again. She asked me how I felt? So I was totally honest and said, in a strange way, it made me love her even more.

Chapter 1

The ultimatum

A few days later she told me he was still flirting and had even asked her if she wanted a promotion to a different department. The position was apparently double her normal salary and benefited from an end of year bonus of well over fifty grand.

I asked her if he'd touched her again and she admitted he had in his office, this time he'd slipped his hand up her skirt and pulled her towards him grabbing her butt. She was clearly embarrassed, but I assured her it was OK and I really wanted to know what else happened as I was incredibly turned on.

Reaching down she felt my erection, then asked if I really wanted to know what else he did? Hugging her tightly I cupped her bottom under her skirt then led her by the hand towards the bedroom. Laying her on the bed, I pulled my jeans off and she saw my aroused manhood standing to attention, so reached out and started fondling me as I knelt in front of her.

"Well... If you really want to know... he was sitting in his chair and I was standing next to him. He'd just told me about the new position in the loan department and slipped his hand between my legs. I was so taken aback and shocked, my mind was racing on how I was going to get away as he was groping me up my skirt over my tights and knickers. Then he pulled me towards him with his other hand on my bum and as he had a really good feel, I nearly peed myself."

That was too much for me and I started ejaculating as we both stared at her hand covered in cum still holding my jerking little cock.

"My God...! It really turns you on doesn't it...!" She exclaimed.

"Yes I know, and I get this weird feeling in my stomach and... I can't explain it but... its like I want you to do it."

"What do you mean Greg, are you saying you want me to have sex with him...!"

"Well... why not... he's married and knows your married, so it'll only be for fun, and you said he was an old guy, so you're not gonna fall in love with him are you...!"

"No... of course not... but... but what about us and..."

I pushed her down on the bed and lifted her skirt, parting and diving down between her legs, I could tell she was just as turned on as me and clearly already wet. Pulling her knickers and tights down to her knees, I pushed her legs up and ate her out like a man possessed, pulling her open with my fingers and licking her pink inner lips until she had the most amazing orgasm.

Pulling her tights all the way off, I climbed on top and tried to penetrate her, but it was too limp and a huge embarrassment. She hugged me and tried to get it up using her fingers and sucking me off, something she'd never done before, but I'd already cum and that was that.

Later that evening we discussed it again and as soon as she told me how he was feeling her up in his office again, I became aroused and we made love properly, but when she told me he'd made her touch his cock as he was exploring between her legs, I fucking lost it and orgasmed again, basically finishing me off for the night.

The following day she came home and said, he'd offered her an ultimatum, either she let him take her to a hotel and spend the afternoon with him or he'd offer the position to someone else. We knew that the double salary and yearly bonus was a life changing opportunity and we could fulfil our dream of moving into a bigger house in a nicer area. And the fact that it was all up front and both knew exactly what was happening, we decided to accept his offer.

She said he wanted to book a hotel the next day, so we made love all evening, as we talked and fantasised about what he'd do. Kirsty cum several times as I pleasured her with my fingers and sucked on her nipples, telling her how I wanted to hear all the naughty details when she came home with his cum still inside her. We'd been trying for a baby for two years and concluded, that either she or I were infertile, but we still wanted a child and this could be an interesting opportunity.

On the day she wore her new red and black lace lingerie set with matching suspenders and sheer black stockings, an elegant knee length dress and looked like she was going to an important business meeting. We kissed and hugged and knowing what was going to happen, I took the day off and stayed at home.

She'd promised to tell me everything when she got home, and even call or text me if she could. So all morning I was trying to make myself busy and wondering, how, what, where and a multitude of questions were going through my mind.

Then just after midday she called saying, he'd booked a room at the Holiday Inn on the A5 at Markyate and she was calling me from the rest room. I told her I knew the hotel, loved her like crazy and wished her luck.

For the next hour and a half, I was wanking like a mad man and cum at least three times...! More than I'd ever managed before and was still pulling away as if I was possessed. The feeling in my gut was indescribable, a mixture of lust, jealousy and love all mixed together. My imagination was running riot, thinking of what they were doing and every scenario I could possibly imagine.

Staring at my phone constantly, begging in my mind for her to call or at least send me a text, but it was silent. The tension was driving me crazy and then she sent a text saying, he'd put her in a taxi and she'd be home in ten minutes. A rush of excitement that I cannot describe flowed over me as I rushed downstairs to wait by the front door.

Chapter 2

Kirsty returns home

As soon as the taxi pulled up, I watched her pay the driver, then elegantly step out and walk up the garden path towards me. Hugging her tightly, she started kissing me and I smelled his cum on her breath. Closing the door, she was immediately feeling for my cock and surprisingly, it came alive, even though I'd strangled the life out of it for the last couple of hours.

Feeling between her legs was the most intense emotional experience ever, soaking wet knickers and caressing her soft thighs above her stockings was out of this world. I managed to slip a finger in and she was fucking full of his spunk. Two fingers and it was driving her wild as she snogged my mouth, biting my lips as I now tasted his spunk on her tongue. We were both in a state of heightened sexual ecstasy and hadn't even managed to get in the lounge, we were still in the hallway on the stairs, pulling her knickers to the side and savouring her cum filled pussy. She in turn was moaning and holding my head between her legs as I licked and sucked on her clit until she screamed she was cumming, jerking and trembling like I'd never seen her do before. Still fully dressed, we climbed the stairs where she collapsed on the bed, so I lay down next to her in a 69, pulling her onto my face, I just couldn't get enough.

"So tell me what happened babe...?"

"He was... Oh My God... He was bloody huge... and he wouldn't stop... I can't remember how many times he made me cum but I was having... like multiple orgasms and it was so intense, I nearly passed out, but he'd change position and start all over again."

"So did he cum in your mouth... I can taste him...?"

"Yes every time he cum, he'd make me take him in my mouth, I never did it before as you know, because you always cum so fast and you're... you know..."

"Too small and yeah... It's OK babe, I understand."

Well he cum inside me then pulled out and turned around, so I was underneath him in a 69, he was between my legs with his long tongue and I was staring at his cock and balls hanging down, I started feeling him and he forced it in my mouth, but then he was making me cum again using his mouth and finger in my bum and he ejaculated in my mouth... there was so much I started coughing and couldn't believe how he could cum so much twice, and it was all over my face. I tried to swallow but he was... Oh God Greg... he was bloody massive."

"How big babe...?"

"Like my bloody forearm...! and it really hurt at first, I thought he was going to split me open, but when I started to cry he stopped trying to force it in and did it more gently, caressing my head and kissing me as he eased the head in and we lay still, then as I got used to the girth, he started rocking slowly, easing it in and out until he was about halfway. I must have cum at least twice while he was doing it like that, but then after about 15 minutes, I was more relaxed and able to let him do it harder."

"So how many times did he cum then...?"

"At least four times and he even wanted to do it in my butt. I was scared as we've never done that before... but he took his time and I was so wet, he lay behind me and holding my leg up, pushed it in. And after the initial pain went away, he was able to get it all in and was fucking me like crazy. He even made me kneel on the floor over the bed as he stood behind me, slapping my bum as he fucked me like a dog. Oh babe it was unbelievable and he must have fucked me more in the bum than in my pussy."

My cock was already jerking as she wanked it faster but nothing was coming out, I was totally dry and she was like a bitch on heat. Exhausted and laying back on the bed, she climbed on my face and pulling her knickers over said dominantly,

"Come on you fucking cuck... clean me up... it was your idea so now you're going to have to do this every time he wants to fuck me with his big cock."

I was in awe at her new found dominance and loving every minute of her talking like that, and every time I tried to speak, she ground her pussy down onto my mouth and told me to shut up and do my job."

She eventually made herself cum by rubbing her clit as I licked her clean and when she eased off I said,

"But you didn't even tell me how it all started...!"

"Hmm m... well I'll tell you when your ready again... OK."

We both burst into laughter, hugging and kissing like we hadn't seen each other in months.

Chapter 3

On the way to the seminar

So that was the first time and she was immediately promoted and had her own office in the bank. It also meant she had to attend more trainings down south, and I was wondering what I was going to do as she said it involved staying the night in a hotel.

A few days later she told me he was still feeling her up at every opportunity and had even fucked her over his desk by locking his office door. Then said she had to attend a weekend seminar in Exeter. I asked if he was going as well and she just smiled and replied,

"Of course...!"

We were making love every evening and I couldn't wait for her to come home and hear what happened and most evenings clean her up. She also told me in detail how he'd seduced her in the hotel that first time, and wanked me off into her mouth, saying how she was actually enjoying the taste.

On the Friday evening we'd arranged for me to receive regular updates by text every time anything happened, and if possible, to leave her phone on so I could listen in. She'd packed her overnight bag as he was picking her up in his car on the Saturday morning at 7 AM.

The first message came through at 7. 30,

"He's playing between my legs and we're on the M4 motorway...!"

At 7.50 she messaged saying,

"He made me play with his cock, but then we got stuck in a traffic jam, now we're driving on the country lanes through the villages."

 I'd already cum fantasising about him playing with her as they drove, with Kirsty laying back with her legs open as he explored and fingered her in the passenger seat.

During the next hour there were no more messages, so I started looking online for herbal remedies for my premature ejaculation. I came across several products and the one that really caught my eye and was at the top of the reviewers list was Volumaxx. I immediately ordered a couple of months supply and then started watching cuckold videos while waiting for her next message.

I didn't hear anything until lunchtime where she called and said, she was in the training and he'd disappeared somewhere and was meeting her at 3.30 when it was finished for the day. I asked her to tell me what happened in the car, so she said, he'd made her recline the passenger seat when they were on the motorway and was stroking her legs over her pantyhose, then made her pull them down so he could finger her as they drove along. Asking if he'd made her cum, she said he did and then he made her lean over and suck him off, but they were then in the traffic jam and had to stop.

She asked me what I'd been doing, so told her about the cuckold videos and that I'd ordered some supplements which pleased her, then she said she'd try to call me later and leave the phone on.

It was well past 7 o'clock and I was going out of my mind. I found out later that he'd taken her to a wine bar and after a couple of bottles of wine, decided to go back to the hotel. Anyway, I received a call at about 8 o'clock and as she didn't answer when I spoke, realised she must be in the room and had left it on the side. I heard her giggling as he was obviously playing with her and then I heard, he was asking her about me. She didn't seem to want to answer, probably as she knew I was listening, but did tell him that I knew she was having sex with him. He then made a comment about me not being able to satisfy her because of my small cock, but she stood up for me by saying, I pleasured her in other ways.

It then went quiet for the longest time and I wondered if they'd left the room, but then I heard her whimper as he must have been doing something.

"Please make me cum with your tongue," I heard her say as she started moaning and sighing. I guessed he was licking between her legs and my erection was bursting to get out. Knowing it would all be over really fast if I started wanking, I tried to hold back and keep listening.

I could only imagine her laying on the bed with her knickers and tights pulled down and him pushing her legs back, licking her shaved slit and anus as she said he really liked doing that before fucking her. She also told me, he was into anal more than anything else, and when I heard her let out a long deep groan, I knew he must have penetrated her and was fucking her arse. The whimpering noises she was making were sending me over the edge and as hard as I tried, as soon as I heard her cum, my cock was jerking and emptying all over my hand.

I heard some movement on the bed and then the moans and sighs started again, this time he must have been fucking her over the side of the bed as I could hear the bed banging against the wall over her moans and his grunting as he shot his cum deep into her arse or pussy, I didn't know where.

Silence again as she must have gone to the bathroom and when she returned he told her to sit on his face and I soon heard him slurping away between her legs as she moaned,

"Oh yes please I love it when you push your tongue in like that."

She was obviously trying to let me know what was going on, I also realised, I'd missed an opportunity to record the event but it was definitely something I'd do in the future so we could listen together when she came home. What I couldn't understand was, why I felt no jealousy... I was definitely in love with her and knew she was with me, but as I listened to him making her cum over and over again, all I felt were, feelings of intense lust and passion. I wanted to be able to satisfy her but no way could I do that with my cock, but I knew I could drive her crazy with my mouth and fingers. And now I'd ordered the supplements, who knows what could happen.

After he'd made her cum again, I heard them moving around and then she was slurping and coughing, he must have been making her go down on him and she was clearly gagging and almost being sick. It went on for quite a while and I could hear everything he said as he was forcing his cock down her throat, telling her to relax and swallow. Then he spat in her mouth and said,

"Come on Kirsty... all the way down now... and then I'm going to fuck you in your tight little arse again."

"Yes... Yes..." she coughed and spluttered as he must have unloaded in her throat and I heard her slide off the bed and run to the bathroom still coughing.

When she came back the phone went dead and I was perturbed

at why she'd switched it off. I quickly looked online for a way to record the calls and was directed to the Google play store where I downloaded a free app.

It was about an hour later when she sent a message saying,

"Hi... he's in the bathroom and I'm so tired... he's been fucking me non stop for the last hour... and I found out he's been taking Viagra."

Half an hour later and she messaged again saying,

"He said he's taking me out to a club, I'll call again later."

The time was 11 PM and I was wondering what the hell was going on, but at 11.20 she called saying she was in a weird nightclub and calling from the rest room. I asked her what she meant by weird? And she said, everyone was dressed up in BDSM or fetish gear and some people were walking around totally naked. I realised he'd taken her to a fetish or swinger club which in a way put my mind at rest.

But then she didn't call of message me until the morning...! I sent her several messages throughout the night but none were answered.

"So what happened babe... Didn't you get my messages...?"

"Yes but after we arrived at the club, he gave me these little pink pills and I couldn't use the phone, my eyes were all over the place and I wasn't able to read the messages."

"What do you mean he gave you some pills... was it ecstasy and are you OK...?"

"Yes I think so... I'm fine but he said everyone used them in the club and it was God I can't describe it... unbelievable... have you ever tried them...?"

"No… can't say as I have… so what do you mean…?"

"Look I have to go now, I'm at the seminar and I didn't get any sleep… He was at it all night and I've got so much to tell you about what happened in the club."

"So how can you go in like that then…?"

"I don't know, but I'm wide awake and still feeling a bit weird but it was so nice and he's in the room. I'll call you later."

She hung up as I paced around wondering what the fuck I was going to do all day.

Chapter 4

On the way home

It was about 12.30 when she called again saying, she had to make an excuse and leave the seminar as she couldn't concentrate and was going back to the room.

Watching videos to kill the time, I couldn't stop thinking about how I was feeling yesterday afternoon, listening to her being brought to orgasm over and over again. And then looking at the time, it was now 3.40 and she'd been quiet for over three hours. Hoping she was on her way back, I opened a bottle of wine and started scanning the porn videos again, then came across an amateur Japanese wife sharing channel. I don't know what it is about Japanese men, but they seem to get turned on by virtually torturing the girls to orgasm as much as possible, using all kinds of toys, vibrators and insertions. And when they start getting into the bondage and forced enemas it gets really weird.

Anyway, I came across this video and the girl was about 25 and absolutely beautiful, she was dressed in a white skirt and knickers, pantyhose and a fluffy pink top. Her husband was looking quite nervous and had invited some friends around, and after several drinks, sat her on his lap and started caressing her. She was also looking apprehensive and it was definitely a home recording as the husband was using his phone and it was jumping all over the place.

But as he caressed her legs and they were all watching and joking, someone else took the phone and started videoing him exposing her knickers and then her tits by pulling her top off. Clearly embarrassed, she tried to cover herself but he was kissing and whispering to her until she relaxed, then let him put his hand in her pantyhose.

Two of his friends moved closer and were on the floor, stroking her legs as he started fingering her inside her knickers. The guy filming was walking around, capturing everything from different angles as the husband then let one of his friends kiss his wife on the mouth as he also explored her breasts still in her white half cup bra. Still in her knickers, the husband was encouraging the other guy still on the floor to stroke her inner thighs and pussy over the pantyhose. She was now starting to relax and enjoy all the hands groping and feeling her all over, and was especially keen on the kissing as her bra was removed and breasts with huge nipples exposed. The husband and friend kissing her mouth were both playing with her tits as the guy on the floor was pulling her pantyhose down over her thighs, then down her legs until he pulled one leg out and pushed her legs apart, delving down and pulling her knickers over so he could lick her pussy with his tongue.

The husband was still holding her on his lap as his three friends were working on her, so he said something in Japanese and they all lifted her off him and lay her down on the sofa. The same guy started snogging her as the others all knelt around, caressing her breasts, legs and hairy pussy. The husband now had the camera and was walking around, videoing his wife moaning and sighing as one of them used two fingers and fingered her to a squirting orgasm. They started undressing as she stared up at her husband about to take a cock in her mouth.

Suddenly the phone rang, I quickly looked at the time and it was just after 4 o'clock, so answered and said hi, but she didn't answer. I heard traffic noise so they were obviously driving, and he was asking her if she enjoyed the club and wanted to try one in London next week. She sounded a bit strange but said she did and was making sighing noises, as if he was playing with her as he drove.

"So what about your husband...? he asked.

"He wanted me to come with you and I agreed to tell him everything... Ooh please... don't tease me.. can we stop and..."

"I see... so he knows you're seeing me and he doesn't mind...!"

"Yes it turns him on."

"Well... What if I come to your home and he can listen in, you have a spare room...?"

"Yes... but I'd have to ask him."

"Yes... I'd like that... I think he'd like to hear you making love with another man. So are you still in love with him...?"

"Of course... Are you in love with your wife...?"

"Yes... but she's not into sex so much these days... She thinks I'm oversexed and let's me have my fun, provided I let her do her own thing and continue her weekly allowance."

I was incredibly turned on and knew he was playing with her as I could hear her sighing every now and then. She must have put the phone in the side pocket so I could listen in. Kirsty was trying to answer him in between making moaning noises but wasn't making any sense. He then told her they were nearly home and was going to stop in the park to finish her off.

I waited for another fifteen minutes and then heard the car stop and he must have been kissing and fingering her still as she was still sighing.

He then said,

"Does he like to make love to you when you come home…?"

"Yes," she whimpered.

"Well I'm going to give him something to remember so get out and lets do it outside."

I thought I was going to hear him fucking her again but after they got out and I heard the car doors close, it was virtually silent.

Fifteen minutes later I heard them get back in and the engine started up. The phone went dead and I was left high and dry again.

Ten minutes later she arrived, and as I stared out the window, he kissed her passionately right outside our house before letting her out the car.

"What the fucks going on…?" I asked as soon as she came in and closed the door.

"He knows you want me to see him, so he said you need to be more active and see what goes on."

"Really…! He said that…?"

"Yes… and he said he wants to come round here and make love in our bed… he said you can watch or listen in but he doesn't want to get into any deep conversation."

"What the fuck is that all about…?"

"He said he doesn't mind you watching but doesn't want to share me."

"Are you fucking joking…! Who the fuck does he think he is…!"

"Oh darling can we go to bed, I'm so horny and I need you to make love with me."

"But didn't he just fuck you in the park…!"

"Yes but you don't understand… I can't stop playing with myself… I think it was the pills and that's why I had to leave the seminar."

"So what happened when you left and what about the club…?"

"Oh Greg… please come to bed and I'll tell you everything."

Chapter 5

The bedroom

We went up stairs and without even undressing I was between her legs on the bed, her gusset was soaking fucking wet and she was full of his spunk. Pulling her tights and knickers down, I could see it still dribbling out as she took her top off and started caressing her tits then rolling her head around. She was obviously not her usual self and was pulling my head into her moaning and said,

"Please babe... make love to me and I'll tell you what happened in the club."

I was still slurping away between her legs but looked up and said,

"Kirsty... l love you so much and just want you to be happy... I know I can't fuck you like him, but I'll do whatever you want OK... just tell me what he did."

"It wasn't just him... because when we went in the club and he gave me the pills... he was like... I can't remember exactly... but he was like a different person... He wasn't dominant or anything... but more like... he wanted to have group sex and was letting another couple join in with us. Oooohhh don't stop babe and push your fingers in harder... he can get four fingers in me and.... Ooh God..."

She let out this long guttural moan as I almost got my whole fucking fist inside her. Grabbing my hand she moaned,

"Yes.. more... push it all in."

"So what else happened babe...?"

"He let this couple start playing with us... we were in a dark room and he was playing with me as we watched all these people on a big bed making love. I was feeling so turned on and it was about an hour after we took the pills. The feeling was amazing and he was sharing me with this couple. She was kissing me and had her hand between my legs as Andreas and her husband were sucking on my boobs and their hands were all over me."

"Andreas...! So that's his name then...?"

"Yes darling... sorry I should have told you but..."

"Never mind... I don't care about his name, only that you enjoy what he does and you tell me everything like we agreed."

"Of course Greg... But it was so naughty and Andreas let the other guy pleasure me on the floor between my legs as he was doing the same to his wife. I was so turned on, I just let him do whatever he wanted. Then we were in a small room and he was fucking the other girl as the husband was inside me. Then we were all doing it together and I was being fucked by Andreas as she was on my face, pressing her pussy down, making me lick between her legs. But his cum was all running out and I know how much you enjoy going down on me now. She was moaning and Andreas was rubbing her clit as she was over my face. Her husband was at the side making me play with his cock and encouraging his wife to cum again."

"Fuck me Kirsty, that's a bloody horny story... so what happened next...?"

"God I can't remember as my mind was all over the place, I couldn't stop playing with myself and he was leading me around... I remember this group of black guys... and he was letting them all play with me and they were taking turns to cum in my mouth."

"What the fuck Kirsty... you're turning into a cum lover now...!"

"I don't know why, but it turns me on so much when I know they're about to cum and when I make them ejaculate, I have to taste it... and they all taste a bit different. Even your cums different to his. He's more salty and really thick, but yours is   clearer and more like coconut juice."

"So did you do anything else with the black guys...?"

It's really weird, I can't remember but maybe... But after that we were in another room and he was fingering my butt and a guy was in front of me sucking my boobs and fingering me. But I was so worked up, they made me cum so hard I was peeing all over his hand...!"

"Fuck me Kirsty.. you're fucking amazing... can I cum in your mouth as well...?"

I quickly changed position so I was kneeling over her head and pulling her legs back in a 69... easing her pussy open, I went back to pleasuring her as she took me in her mouth. Sucking it hard, she even managed to get my balls in and the feeling was so unbelievable I shot my load as she took it all, smiling and rolling them around in her mouth. Still as horny as hell, she wanted me to keep trying to get my whole hand inside her, as if she wanted to stretch herself as much as possible.

"So can get his whole cock in you now...?" i asked staring at her gapping pink pussy that was absolutely delicious and drenched in my saliva and his cum still oozing out.

"Not all of it... but he likes doing it in my bottom more... he said he can get it in deeper as he's quite long and really wide. So you want him to come round to the house then...?"

"Hmm m... I'd love to see you making love with him but he sounds a bit too arrogant for my liking."

"I think it's because he's from Brazil and I must admit, he's very dominant and not much of a talker, but he said you'd probably want to watch him making love to me. You don't have to talk to him or anything, and you can video me and we can watch it together later."

"So how do you feel about him now then...?"

"What do you mean...?"

"I mean... What if I said I didn't want you to see him anymore...?"

"But then I'd lose my job at the bank and... really...! you don't want me to see him anymore..?"

"No I'm not saying that babe, I just wanted to know if you felt any different about me after this last weekend doing all that with him."

"Oh darling... I love you and we agreed I'd tell you everything...!"

"Yes I know... And I'm sorry if I upset you... it's just that I was going out of my mind at times... especially when I didn't know what was going on and it was hours between calls...!"

"I'm sorry darling... But I was trying to be discrete and not let him know I was calling you... but he knows now, and that's why he suggested coming around to the house."

"Coming here to the house...! So what about his wife then... does she know what he gets up to...?"

"I think so... He said she's not interested in clubbing or sex anymore."

"Maybe she's in her fifties like him...!"

"No... he said she's a lot younger than him... in her early thirties I think."

"Hmm... that's a bit weird...!"

We lay together as I was still playing between her legs and asking her more questions but she was more interested in me trying to fist her than talking.

Sunday was a bit more relaxing and she was back to her normal self, we went out for lunch and spent the day walking in the countryside near our house.

Chapter 6

Two weeks later

F ast forward two weeks and we both realised that things had progressed far quicker than we'd imagined, and our lives had changed dramatically. He was fucking her everyday in his office at the bank and she'd tell me all about it when she got home. My supplements had arrived and we were both impressed at the volume of seminal fluid I could produce and more importantly, that I could stay up longer. Kirsty had developed a real taste for sperm and was letting me cum in her mouth as I savoured his cum mixed with her juices every evening. However, even though I was harder and able to stay up longer, nothing was going to help me with my size.

He'd arranged to take her to a new club at the weekend, and she asked me if she could bring him home and stay the night. I said OK because I needed to see what he was like and even more interestingly, how she was able to take his massive cock.

She said they'd be having some ecstasy again and this week he was taking her to a private swingers club in Hampstead, North London.

We spent the morning together in town, shopping for something sexy to wear as she wanted to look her best and picked out a white see through negligee that almost covered her bottom and a matching G-string, also a black leather basque that forced her breasts up and together, making them look bigger with her nipples poking out with a pair of tight black leather knickers.

He'd also told her to get a nice butt plug, so we found one with a crystal diamond on the end and a couple of different sized ones in black rubber. One of them was fucking huge, of which she said she really wanted because it was like his cock...!
I was in awe that she could take anything like that inside her at all.

On the Saturday afternoon, she called him up to ask what was appropriate to wear and he told her the negligee as it was a smaller gathering of mainly couples, then asked her if she was inviting him home later that evening? She told him, I had agreed and would be in the spare room.

So all was arranged and he picked her up at 8 o'clock. Hugging me at the door, I felt that strange feeling in my gut again and was already getting aroused. She promised to text me more often, and I said I'd keep out the way when she came home, but to leave the bedroom door slightly ajar. She wore a long coat over her skimpy outfit and was shaved smooth with the new butt plug inserted.

I didn't get a message as they were driving and the first one came through when they arrived.

"Hi... We've arrived and it's a nice apartment building in an exclusive area. There are 5 other couples and 4 very well endowed black guys walking around naked except for wrist and neck collars serving drinks LOL. They also offered us some pills and he's been feeling my bum and plug saying how sexy I look this evening. Xxx."

It was about an hour later when she sent the next message.

"Can't focus very well, it's the ecstasy I think and I'm feeling so horny. Tell you everything later... I'm OK but he wants us to join another couple in one of the bedrooms and told me to put the phone away... Sorry babe X."

I wasn't happy as I was expecting regular updates, so opened the computer and started browsing videos.

It was just past 1 AM when she called, saying they were on their way home and to wait in the spare room. I was already in bed and unbeknown to Kirsty, had set up a secret webcam our bedroom to record everything.

Twenty minutes later and I heard them coming in the front door and she led him straight up the stairs to our bedroom. Laying in bed, I'd already opened the webcam on my phone and was watching in anticipation as she led him in and threw her coat on the chair, still wearing her see through negligee. He was nothing like I'd imagined, I expected a tall, dark and attractive or handsome man with, but he was quite unattractive, short and stocky. He didn't say a word, but pushed her down on our bed and went down on her, pinning her legs back so she was almost bent double. She immediately started moaning and rolling her head around as he was giving her a really intense licking. Obviously trying to make her cum and make as much noise as possible, knowing I was listening in the spare room.

I was wanking furiously and had already cum a couple times during the evening, waiting for her to send a message but watching and listening to her moans like this was unbelievable and sent me over the edge so quickly, I was now running on empty and hardly anything was coming out.

It didn't take long before she was jerking and trying to push him off as her climax was so intense. He then let her legs down as he stripped off and I saw his huge member for the first time. He was at least a foot long and fat like her forearm. Climbing on the bed he knelt by her head as she looked up at it, he was rubbing the end all over her face, teasing her by slapping it on her cheek and forehead before letting her pull him into her mouth.

Hand between her legs, he started forcing his fat stubby fingers in making her moan as she took his cock head in her mouth. How she managed to get it in was beyond me, it was like the size of a small apple. But somehow she was licking and slurping around while massaging his balls.

I was so fucking turned on watching him bring her off and even though I'd just cum, luckily I was still hard because of the supplements. And when I heard her coughing and gagging, rt was obvious he'd just ejaculated down her throat. The moans and sounds were out of this world and knowing that, they both knew I was listening, was an even bigger turn on.

Then as he rolled over onto his back, I saw her wiping her mouth, she must had swallowed the rest as she was licking her lips just like when she did it to me earlier. Pulling her on top, she looked towards the door but I was watching on webcam so she couldn't see me. Gripping his huge member, she lowered herself down as the head slipped inside. Then as he pulled her down, she closed her eyes and let out a long moan that was almost a scream. But she was clearly enjoying being stretched to the limit, and as he moved her up and down by holding her hips, she hugged his head and again stared at the gap in the door, probably wondering why I wasn't standing there watching.

I decided to get out of bed and go take a peek and she immediately saw me as I stood by the gap stroking my cock. Her eyes were big and wide and had a strange look on her face, I could tell she was high, rolling her head around as he penetrated her deeper and deeper until she was wailing and screaming,

"I'm cumming... I'm cumming... ohhh God...!"

Jerking like I'd never seen her do before, she was impaled almost all the way on his cock as he held her down, grunting and still bucking underneath her, trying to prolong her spasms.

"I hope we gave your husband a good show... Tell him he can come in and he can watch from the chair," he said all matter or factly.

Looking up at me she indicated with her head to come in, reluctantly I opened the door and stood in the doorway staring at them still holding my cock that was unbelievably still hard but they probably couldn't even so it.

"Are you OK darling...? Err...this is Andreas... and Andreas, this is Greg my husband," she said staring at me with wide eyes to see my reaction.

"Your wife is very beautiful and she tells me you like to watch," he said.

"Yes... I'm quite new to all this but I suppose I do."

"And did it turn you on watching me make her scream and orgasm and then unloading my sperm in her mouth...? Hmm m... truly a sexy wife you have here... So you want to watch as I make her orgasm again yes...?"

"Err... Yes why not... I've never heard her cum like that before...!"

"Well Greg... she's been well and truly fucked this evening at the party... and I especially like it when she's sitting on another guy like this and I enter her back passage, then we fuck her together as she has multiple orgasms."

"So your wife isn't into it then...?" I asked.

"Not anymore, she was at first but women... I cannot understand them... but I don't want to talk about her. If you want me to pleasure your wife... I will be more than happy... She's still high and incredibly horny, so I'm going to show you how she likes it in her other hole... then you can go back to your room and listen in as we make love some more."

I sat down and didn't answer as he seemed to be getting pissed off with talking and had rolled Kirsty off as he sat up and he slapped her arse, telling her to kneel on the bed and pull herself open. Incredibly, she just did as he asked and had her head buried in the pillows, pulling her own butt cheeks apart. I could see her butt plug was gone and her anus was nowhere near as tight as I remembered but gapping slightly. She'd obviously been well fucked there and was still gagging for more.

Climbing on the bed behind her, he first lubricated it up by plunging in her pussy, then eased out and aimed it in her other hole. Turning her head so she could see me, I saw her say to me, "I love you," as he eased in, making her arch her back and bite her bottom lip sighing loudly. He was in at least half way and immediately started humping faster, and within a few more strokes was about three quarters of the way in as she gripped and bit the pillows with closed eyes.

He was like a big stocky bear and covered in hair, not fat, and his body was almost twice as wide as me. His arms and legs were short and muscular and made Kirsty look tiny in comparison.

As he groped at her hanging breasts and grunting like a cave man, it was like I was in a surreal movie, wanking and watching my wife being anally pounded, and as soon as she started jerking and screamed she was cumming again, I was ejaculating and spurting my last few drops of spunk onto my hand.

When he eased out, she collapsed on the bed, eyes closed and hugging the pillow.
I got up and walked towards the door as he smiled and gave me a thumbs up. She didn't see me leave, but I made sure to leave the door ajar so I could hear what happened next.

Back in the spare room, it was eerily quiet for a good 30 minutes, on cam I saw he was laying next to her, stroking her hair as she was playing with and kissing his cock, and then he pulled her on top and was fucking her again. And every time I heard her moan, it made my gut go all weird and even though my balls were totally drained, my cock was coming back to full hardness proving that sex is definitely in the mind. It brought back the memory of a joke I heard, a group of monks had decided to cut off their cocks, so as to become pure and celibate... But the old monk telling the story said, what they didn't understand was that sex and desire is not in their physically severed cocks... It is still in their minds and now will drive them crazy with lust and feelings they can do nothing to appease.

So as I lay in bed, listening and pleasuring myself gently, using my own saliva as it was getting very red and sore, the door opened and Kirsty walked in. Pleased and surprised, I patted the bed, so she came over and without saying a word slid in next to me. Kissing me passionately, I could taste and smell his cum on her breath as she reached down to fondle me at the same time.

I did the same and slipped my hand down between her legs, but it felt so different, she was so wet and gapping, his spunk mixed with her sticky white cum was running down my fingers. Sliding on top, she tried to get my cock in, but she was so opened up, I couldn't feel a thing and it kept slipping out. She then pushed the covers off and turned around in a 69 kneeling over my face.

I was in heaven as she lowered herself down, letting me taste her fluids as she took my cock and balls in her mouth. Pulling her wide open, I savoured and pleasured her like we did a few nights ago. She was trying to bring me off so I could cum in her mouth, but I moaned that I'd already cum four times and was empty, but she still continued, rolling my balls around in her mouth and even forced a finger in my anus. I'd never been so turned on and she was doing things I'd never even dreamed of asking her to do before.

But as she started grinding her pussy down on my mouth, I knew she was about to cum again and started sucking and licking on her clit really fast. I started ejaculating but nothing was coming out, Kirsty was giggling and then she exploded and I felt her squirting in my mouth...! Knowing it was probably the ecstasy, I didn't push her away, but lapped it up like a thirsty dog. It wasn't a lot, just a few spurts but she was clearly more turned on than I'd ever seen her before.

Easing off and laying next go me, we heard the front door close downstairs and a few minutes later him driving away.

"It's OK... He told me to come and see you... he said he knows what you were feeling and needed after hearing us make love," she said hugging me tightly.

"So he's not staying the night then…?"

"Darling… It's 5 AM and nearly daylight…! Shall we stay here or do you want to come back in our room…?

"No… let's stay here… This is my room now."

I hope you enjoyed this short story.

Most of my stories are raw and personal and about actual people, so if you like my writing style, and stories about Husband or Wife sharing, Wife watching, BDSM, Cuckold, Swinger and Fetish clubs, Dogging and many other fetishes...

The FULL LIST of all my other stories can be found on my

Amazon Author page

Amazon.com/author/danteserotica

Or on Amazon search for: DANTE X

Register on my website to get the heads up on all my new releases and sample excerpts on the blog.

Website: www.DantesErotica.uk

Dante x

Sample of Dante's books available on Amazon, iTunes and Audible.

Steppingley Manor (Private Members Club) series

Steppingley Manor

Dantes Erotica - Private Members Club

Dantes Erotica - Yasmin's Abduction

Waterworld Thailand - The Girl on the beach

The Navigator - An Erotic Sailing Adventure

Bangkok and the Vampires of the night

Japanese Escort

Transsexuals and Katoys in Thailand

Dogging with Dave

Insatiable

Asuka's cuckold Induction

Ladyboys - 10 different stories

British Indian wife 2 book set

Asian Wife Series of 14 books

Erotic Story Collection 1, 2, 3, 4 and 5

The Man on the Train

The Man in the Park

Dangerous Game – Wife watching and sharing

The German Inventor

Living on a boat

The Landlords Tales

Swinging and Wife Sharing

The Arrangement

Shonie's Watersports Parties

Jinn - Egyptian Adventure with Supernatural Horror

Adult Theatre Lover – Cinema Groping with Strangers

Erotic Lucid Dreaming – A technique for seduction

Abduction and Escape (Two book series)

Sexless marriage led to our naughty game

Revenge on the Bitch

Abducted and Addicted in Hong Kong

Fat Bastard Seduces my Wife

Something about Jasmine

Full Title List on www.Danteserotica.uk

Printed in Great Britain
by Amazon

77053813R00031